Carrots, Cre

Flashes fı

Edited by Black Pear Press

With contributions by the entrants in the 2021
Worcestershire Literary Festival
Flash Fiction Competition

Thanks and acknowledgements to Judges:
Prof. Rod Griffiths
Dr. Tony Judge

This anthology is brought to you by
The Worcestershire Literary Festival
Flash Fiction Team www.worcslitfest.co.uk

Carrots, Cream, and Death
Flashes from LitFest
Worcestershire Literary Festival
Flash Fiction Competition Anthology 2021

First published in November 2021
by Black Pear Press
www.blackpear.net

Compiled & edited by:
Black Pear Press

ISBN 978-1-913418-52-6

Cover Design by Black Pear Press

Anthologies from Black Pear Press

Short Stories:

On the Day of the Dead and Other Stories
A collection of stories is taken from selected entries to the second Black Pear Press Short Story Competition, which took place during 2016.
Paperback ISBN: 978-1-910322-41-3
eBook ISBN: 978-1-910322-42-0

Seaglass and Other Stories
A collection of short stories from various authors in the first Black Pear Press short story competition 2014.
Paperback ISBN: 978-1-910322-14-7
eBook ISBN: 978-1-910322-15-4

Short Stories from Black Pear—Volume 1
A collection of short stories from Worcestershire-based authors including humour, true life, science fiction, horror and some almost impossible to categorise.
Paperback ISBN: 978-0-9927755-0-6
eBook ISBN: 978-0-9927755-2-0

Flash Fiction:

Her Final Goodbye—Flashes from LitFest
Winners and selected entries from the Worcestershire LitFest & Fringe Flash Fiction Competition 2020.
Paperback ISBN: 978-1-910322-25-0

The Jar Thief—Flashes from LitFest
Winners and selected entries from the Worcestershire LitFest & Fringe Flash Fiction Competition 2019.
Paperback ISBN: 978-1-910322-17-8

Sacrifice—Flashes from LitFest
Winners and selected entries from the Worcestershire LitFest & Fringe Flash Fiction Competition 2018.
Paperback ISBN: 978-1-910322-89-5

Wired—Flashes from LitFest
Winners and selected entries from the Worcestershire LitFest & Fringe Flash Fiction Competition 2017.
Paperback ISBN: 978-1-910322-53-6
eBook ISBN: 978-1-910322-54-3

A Cache of Flashes 2016
Winners and selected entries from the Worcestershire LitFest & Fringe Flash Fiction Competition 2016.
Paperback ISBN: 978-1-910322-39-0
eBook ISBN: 978-1-910322-40-6

A Stash of Flashes 2015
Winners and selected entries from the Worcestershire LitFest & Fringe Flash Fiction Competition 2015.
Paperback ISBN: 978-1-910322-20-8
eBook ISBN: 978-1-910322-21-5

Fifty Flashes of Fiction
Winners and selected entries from the Worcestershire LitFest & Fringe Flash Fiction Competition 2014.
Paperback ISBN: 978-1-910322-10-9
eBook ISBN: 978-1-910322-11-6

Flashes of Fiction 2013
Winners and selected entries from the Worcestershire LitFest & Fringe Flash Fiction Competition 2013.
Paperback ISBN: 978-0-9927755-1-3
eBook ISBN: 978-0-9927755-3-7

A Flash of Fiction 2012
Winners and selected entries from the Worcestershire LitFest & Fringe Flash Fiction Competition 2012.
Paperback ISBN: 978-1-2911065-6-5

eBook and paperback first published by Crown East Publishing 2012 now available via Black Pear Press

Competition Winners

Coronavirus restrictions during 2021 prevented the festival from being held in the usual manner, so, this year, the Worcestershire Literary Festival Flash Fiction Competition 2021 and the Flash Fiction Team announced the winners at the online launch of 2021's virtual Worcestershire LitFest on 6th June.

The top ten flashes (alphabetically by title) were:

Caravaggio's Virgin—Roz Levens
Carrots, Cream, and Death—Jamie D Stacey
Filling the Void—Sue Armstrong
Home, Alone—Helen Beckett
No Baby Talk—Susan Howe
On the Properties of Glass—Jamie D Stacey
Password Not Recognised—Hedy Lewis
The Apple Doesn't Fall Far from the Tree—Polly Stretton
To Kimberley Dene, A Girl He Once Bothered—James Mason
Turncoat—Hedy Lewis

From these, Judges Rod and Tony awarded:

First prize to Jamie D Stacey—*Carrots, Cream, and Death*
Second prize to Helen Beckett—*Home, Alone*
Third prize to Sue Armstrong—*Filling the Void*

These stories are the first that appear in this anthology, followed by the rest of the shortlist and then other entries selected by the BPP team.

Introduction

We celebrate the tenth year of the Worcestershire LitFest and Fringe flash fiction anthology. The competition, founded by Lindsay Stanberry-Flynn in 2011, continues to be a popular event in the annual flash fiction calendar. In 2021 we heard the sad news that Lindsay had died after a prolonged illness. She will be greatly missed as a friend to the Worcestershire literary scene, a champion of flash fiction and a talented published writer of novels and short fiction.

The anthology contains selected flash fictions entered in the competition, and we at Black Pear Press feel privileged to be asked by LitFest to compile, edit and publish it.

Prof. Rod Griffiths and Dr. Tony Judge read all the anonymised entries and made the tough decision to select winners.

The judges look for well-written and entertaining stories. They always say 'flash fiction is a difficult craft to master' because writing a story with a beginning, middle and end, within 300 words, is quite a feat. For a flash to be satisfying, every word must count.

Our winners more than met the judges' expectations, as you will see when you read their pieces in this anthology. Congratulations to Jamie D Stacey, who took first prize with 'Carrots, Cream and Death'. Helen Beckett gained second prize with 'Home, Alone'. Sue Armstrong took third prize with 'Filling the Void'.

Thank you to every entrant for sending your flashes in to this competition. We know that it takes courage to have your writing judged by others. A final thank you to all the LitFest flash fiction team for your sterling work behind the scenes and, in particular, for rising to the extra challenge of holding a competition during the 2021 coronavirus lockdown.

Black Pear Press Limited
www.blackpear.net

Contents

Carrots, Cream, and Death—Jamie D Stacey

From the moment we are born, we begin to die. Mum tells me this, holding my hand, big fat tears falling like wingless angels before the procession.

I want to bake a cake. A carrot cake, with extra cream to hug the fluffy sponge—the way Nana likes it best. I'm walking beside her now. It's odd to walk with someone while they're sleeping. *I want to bake a cake—that always wakes me up*, I tell Mum, but she's not listening.

Someone plays the piano and it sounds like the colour grey.

I want to paint. A big bright rainbow for Nana. She loves colour—she never uses grey and her hair is purple pansies. Everyone stands, hugging bibles and I wonder if there'll be a miracle—the roof parting, clouds running, sun shining.

We sing a song I don't know. It sounds grey. I sing, anything, shouting so Nana will hear and maybe wake up. Mum shakes her head, but she's not listening.

Back in my room I tell myself *Nana is just sleeping*, but when I hit my pillow the tears don't lie. Wingless angels. I go downstairs to where the small rectangular box we've inherited sits. She's been cremated; she is dead in a million pieces. I ask God how He will put her back together again. I pick up the box, try to feel the weight of her and it's surprisingly heavy.

She's stuck in a cage, I tell Mum, but she's not listening.

From the moment we are born, we begin to die. I'm thinking of this as I pour the pieces of Nana into the garden. *She'll live again*, I tell Mum whose scent is carrot and cream. *Next spring we'll see flowers of her, all the colours of the rainbow.*

Home, Alone—Helen Beckett

Cath knocked, louder this time. The noise bounced off the door and the garden path before drifting away down the deserted street. She stared at the overflowing carrier bags pressed against her feet, noticing the beads of moisture that had started to run down the box of frozen fish.

She peered in through the lounge window but his favourite armchair was empty. With a sinking feeling, she hammered on the door, then tried the handle. She nearly fell into the hall as the door swung open.

'He's not here, Jen. I've looked all over the house…'

'Don't panic, Cath. He's probably gone to meet Mum.'

'But why would he…?'

She turned and ran down the street. Ahead of her, she could just make out a figure, shuffling slowly towards the bus stop. In her relief, she shouted at the elderly man. 'How many times do I have to tell you not to go out. And where's your mask?'

He grimaced with the effort of remembering. 'I just wanted to meet your mother off the bus.'

'Oh, Dad!' She hugged him.

Taking his arm, she led him back to the house, unpacked the shopping, then flicked on the kettle.

'Do you want a cup of tea, Dad?'

'Yes, and make one for Mum too please love.'

She opened the cupboard door and took out a single mug, wiping away the tears that glistened on her cheeks.

Filling the Void—Sue St. John

Right from the start she'd said she didn't want children. 'Too much time and too much money.' He'd gone along with it and devoted his life to his work. Now both retired with a lot more time and more money than needed, she felt a pull at her heartstrings for the life not lived. It was too late now.

She busied herself with the WI and the Gardening Club. He discovered golf. Every day he'd put his Calloway clubs into the back of his 4x4 and disappear all day only returning home for a G&T and supper.

This wasn't what she'd planned, where was their time together?

'If you can't beat 'em, join 'em,' she rallied and secretly enrolled for lessons at the municipal golf course. As soon as she knew she could drive, chip, pitch and putt satisfactorily she went to the Royal Bassingbourne Golf Club. 'A joint membership please, with my husband Mr Cripps.' But there was no Mr Cripps at the RBGC. The Membership Secretary looked embarrassed. 'What had he uncovered?' he said to his wife later.

She had no idea where she was driving her Mercedes open top sports. She couldn't go home, not yet. It was all too raw for the inevitable show down.

Finding herself in an unknown, run down part of town she pressed the switch to deploy the automatic roof. To her right she saw a sign: 'Bassingbourne Children's Home'. A group of young children were giggling as a man was trying to play football with his legs tied together. As he stumbled and fell the children poured on top of him shrieking with delight as he tried to tickle them off.

And there, lying down on a playing field, roaring with laughter as his arms flailed around, was Mr Cripps.

Caravaggio's Virgin—Roz Levens

I'd never met anyone like him before.

'You need a job, girl,' my mother said. 'There's this chap up near the bell tower looking for an artist's model. You could do that, you're bone idle, never move a muscle unless you have to—you may as well make some money out of it.'

So I went. He was at the top of the campanile. Thirty-seven stairs. Nobody mentioned that. Red and puffing, I banged on his door.

'Signor Caravaggio?'

He looked at me.

I'd never been looked at so thoroughly before. He looked at ALL of me. Slowly. Deliberately.

I was embarrassed. I wanted to cross my arms across my body to protect myself from his searching gaze. But I didn't. What've I got to be ashamed about?

'You'll do.'

He didn't ask my name, or why I'd come.

'Put this on.'

He threw a bundle of red at me. I held it up, trying to work out which way up it went.

'Get a move on, there's a screen over there, girl. You'll get used to it. No room for modesty in an artist's model.'

'And bare feet—' he yelled, over the top of the screen.

There wasn't enough material, but I draped myself best as I could, and padded, barefoot, back into the room.

'Lie there.'

So I did what I do best. I lay still, eyes shut, for hour after hour, days on end. His soft voice caressed me, telling me I was beautiful, the best model ever, that he loved me...

When I saw the final painting, I regretted letting him have his way, of course I did. I'm not a loose woman—but the cheek of the man; I looked like some drowned tart.

Never trust a man with a paintbrush.

No Baby Talk—Susan Howe

The young woman sitting opposite on the bus hasn't stopped texting since we boarded twenty-five minutes ago. Her child, a little girl by the colour of her pushchair, sits quietly, gazing around and taking everything in. She has fluffy hair and round blue eyes alight with intelligence and curiosity. She's facing away from her mother and occasionally cranes her neck to try to catch her attention, waving her pudgy little hands in the air. I lean forwards and catch one, jiggle it about and tell her she's beautiful. Her eyes widen, then she rewards me with a gummy grin. Her mother doesn't look up but pulls the pushchair a little closer to her seat so that I can't quite reach. The elderly man next to her winks at me and shrugs.

The child's waves become more frantic as she tries to wriggle down and escape the harness. Her reddening face crumples and I steel myself to the cry that will undoubtedly rip forth. When it finally comes, it is more of a whimper than a scream. Frowning, the mother rummages in her bag, pulls out a dummy and stuffs it in her daughter's mouth. Her phone pings and the thumbs busy themselves once again.

I watch as the baby sucks the rubber teat. Her eyelids grow heavy and the long feathery lashes settle on her cheeks. Between messages the young woman glances down at her baby and I want to ask her, 'Why did you have this wonderful child if you weren't interested in her?'

I don't, of course. It's none of my business. But my heart aches as I gather my shopping and step off the bus, afraid she won't even notice when the light goes out in those remarkable eyes.

On the Properties of Glass—Jamie D Stacey

Glass is transparent, a property which leaves it open to the outside world

You told me, with the marble moon and myriad beads of stars, that you saw right through to my silicate soul. You took my hand and I let you kiss me; let you tell me everything will be alright. I believed every word, every sharp-tipped letter that fell from your mouth.

Glass is an excellent insulator against heat, electricity, and electromagnetic radiation… as well as having a high resistance to the transmission of sound

How many smudges and stains have you left behind from your mouth pressed firmly against me? I let you hold me for longer than I probably should have; when you came back late from work, the pub, her… In your arms I took all the excess heat burning from you, and I didn't hear the shouts on the other side from friends and family telling me that this was probably not a good idea.

Glass is weather resistant, withstanding the backlash of the rain, wind, and sun

Rain, pelting. Hitting, hurting. Fill up this empty vase with all your weather. Wiping the rain caught on my cheeks, I told myself I could brace another storm and we would be okay.

Glass is a hard material, it has a great resistance against an applied load; however, it is also brittle, breaking immediately when subjected to sudden force

Hearts are squeezed, stretched, stressed until they break in the middle and at the ends. That's how you left me, pain of glass with enough holes pierced through it to spell out a broken heart.

A reminder: glass is forged in the hottest of temperatures

With enough heat you can fix any glass; shape this liquid body into something new.

I am stronger than you thought.

Password Not Recognised—Hedy Lewis

I'm reading the inscription for the ninth time today. I've not even had breakfast yet. Now that I check, it's closer to lunch. Time is tricky these days, speeding by unnoticed or stopping completely if it catches you watching.

Before, I rattled through life like an empty carriage. Hurtling along, taking corners on two wheels, fuelled by a need to keep busy and a lack of patience. It's how we met.

I'd tried to open the project file twice before I threw the laptop across the helpdesk at you.

'Password not recognised,' I'd huffed. You smiled the storm out of me. That was the password to Life With You.

For nearly fifteen years everything felt calmer, better. For thirteen of them I hoped, then nagged, for a proposal. Now I wonder if that drew attention to us. You, on one knee, in Paris, the fireworks at our wedding. The ring engraved with my first words to you. Did somebody see and decide it was too good to last?

They found you at your desk, head on your arms. Thinking, they assumed, but time ticked by until eventually someone checked. It wasn't dramatic, you never were. I used to call you Steady Eddie, mostly out of frustration, convinced you slowed me down. Now the prospect of being without you is terrifying. A kite without a string.

Life now is stationary. Stalled. I forget you're not here, mugs of cold tea litter the house, waiting for you. I can't pour them away. Your shirts are still in the washing machine. I can't touch them when they're empty of you.

Now I'm supposed to run program 'Life Without You', but that's password protected too. Try as I might I can't get it to open. Thing is, I don't think I want it to.

The Apple doesn't Fall Far from the Tree—Polly Stretton

'What are you hiding in your pocket? Show me.'

'No,' Emma pulls away, 'it's mine.'

Mum grabs the letter; it begins to tear. They both clutch the crinkled paper until it's plucked away, held in Mum's grip.

'We don't have secrets.'

Mum's glance is cold, harsh. Emma shrinks back from Mum's rage, then lunges for the letter. Misses. She avoids a sideswipe and runs upstairs to her room. She loathes this woman "Mum".

'Come down here, stop bawling.' Mum flicks at the letter in her hand, '"My angel, I love you".'

Why does Mum hate her so?

Emma thinks of Josh, who wrote the letter. She hears Dad's key in the door and knows Mum's face will now be smooth, she'll pat her hair, simper, help him off with his damp raincoat.

Emma wants to hug Dad, feel the roughness of his tweed jacket.

'What d'you think was in her pocket?' Mum hands Dad his drink. Whisky laced with cigar scent reaches Emma.

'What was in your pocket, girlie?'

'A letter, Dad, it's mine.'

'...she's too young to have letters from boys.' Mum gives Dad a look. Momentarily, it seems the 'anything for a quiet life' attitude will prevail. But he looks hard at his wife.

'Is it addressed to you, Joan?'

'She hid it.'

'You'd best give it back.'

Emma peers through the gap, Dad has his arms around Mum.

'You've a short memory,' Dad says. 'Remember my letter? Your Mum didn't take it, did she?'

'...different, George. I'm different...didn't have her mother...the apple doesn't fall far from the tree.'

'Stop, she'll hear you. We wouldn't have her but for...'

Big fat tears roll down Mum's face, Emma knows they're not real. It's Friday. Mum will save her revenge for Monday.

Emma will be ready.

To Kimberley Dene, A Girl He Once Bothered—James Mason

'Somehow, you bother me,' she said and he carried that sentence home as a prize. She followed him everywhere. He was pursued by the sound of her popping her chewing gum, her flower market smell of flavoured lip balm and deodorant, the Chinese puzzle of her laugh. Or, at least, she appeared every time he closed his eyes. The tight way her acid wash jeans moved against her thighs, the loose way her sleeveless T-shirt hung down when she leaned forward to whisper wicked things with her friends, set something off inside him. He felt the way pigeons feel when, all at once, they launch up in a single crowd: that clattering, close panic.

After what he felt was a thousand years had flown by and it was Friday again, he brushed his hair into a hundred different styles and dowsed himself in his father's Old Spice like he was trying to put out flames, then rushed upstairs and washed it all off (and brushed his hair eight different ways again).

Her parents' house was the other side of the estate. He walked there in double time. He stopped on the corner of her street, outside Wakeem's Regency corner shop. Then, unnerved, ran halfway home. Leaning against a lamppost, his heart rattled like a quid in a charity tin. He daubed two wet marks on his chinos where he wiped his hands. He bothered her, he told himself. And this time he got right to her front door, close enough that he could see where the gilt had worn off the brass number 2 screwed into it. He raised his hand. Paused. Found he couldn't knock. He scuttled home. Next Saturday, he watched her, plump and mysterious, folding herself into the bucket seat of Kev Price's snot green Ford Capri.

Turncoat—Hedy Lewis

She walked home through the wrong part of town. He followed. In the right part of town, her taxi home money paid for one more Manhattan and the hope that the bartender might make a move. He hadn't.

Here were empty houses, shopfronts boarded up. A sleeping bag, a pile of cardboard. All quietly watched her. When she stumbled off her heel, his hand caught her elbow. 'It's not safe here.'

'I'm aware of that, thank you, goodnight.' She sped up, as did he.

'I'll escort you, until it's safe.'

'I've no money.'

'I'm not after your money. Or your phone. Or those pearl earrings. But my associates might be.'

Her keys slipped between her fingers.

'I'm guessing the earrings were confirmation gifts?'

Surprised, she glanced at him. Blackened fingers raked through greasy locks. 'And I'm guessing you weren't born into hardship?'

He laughed like last winter's snow, deep and crisp and even. 'No. I chose this.'

'Spare any change?' a shadowy hand lurched out. She pulled her ankles away and her collar up.

'You can't turn your collar up against the world,' he said. 'However hard done to you feel, your privilege can always help others.'

'Did throwing your privilege away help others?'

Streetlights arrived. A hipster food court, an urban brewery. He stopped, some unseen line he couldn't cross. 'You'll be okay from here.'

Finally, she saw him, cold beneath thin clothes. Eyes tired, because he always slept with one open. Her coat slipped from her shoulders.

'It'll keep you warm.'

Taking it, he watched until she disappeared, shivering back to her bedsit.

Come morning, breakfast TV hides the silence. She stares, open-mouthed, as camera flashes dazzle the press conference. The headline reads 'Billionaire philanthropist returns after search to "find humanity".'

On the screen, he wears her coat.

4JG—Paul Johnson

Dreamed about Ballard again last night. I was in a cab, I'd either stolen it or been born in it (you know how dreams are) but I received a call to go and pick up a fare at one of the three high rises that puncture the city's western skyline. On the third beep of the horn JG emerged from a works elevator, he was wearing a sports jacket, trainers and what looked like freshly ironed jeans. He explained that he had one day back on earth and wanted to see how things had panned out, basically just drive him around. I pulled out onto a filter lane and moments later we were merging with the city's one-way nervous system. JG sat quietly in the back, silent save for whenever an ambulance went past when he murmured 'service vehicle'.

Worcester isn't really anyone's idea of a dystopian nightmare but we sat for a while on Friar St where Ballard gazed approvingly up at the spiralling concrete edifice that is the old Gifford car park, seemingly held together by fly posters and graffiti. On the Cross he stood in full salute to a CCTV camera (and which nodded in recognition) whilst above it gulls circled and screamed out, haloed by halogen, true protectors of his legacy. We dined at Browns where over a chocolate dessert JG examined my mobile phone, tentatively at first, then excitedly before returning it reluctantly, food untouched. As it got dark we headed east out of the city and parked up on a slip road near Motorway 5; Ballard wanted to listen to the sirens and feel the darkness ripple. At no point did he open his window. I dropped him off near the station, the only tip he gave me was to get some sleep.

A Life in Métro—Fritz Cavelle

Pierre-Marie de Villiers was a creature of habit. He made the same journey every day. He took Lines 6, 10 and 4—Passy to Grenelle to Odéon to St Michel—arriving in good time for midday Mass.

He'd taken this same route as a child to sing soprano in Notre Dame's fine boys' choir. Later he'd stop at Odéon for the Sorbonne to study Economics and Politics. He would have taken Theology and the cloth if Line 2 to Pigalle's girls had not left him without a moral high-ground.

In the 1930's he had ventured on Line 3 to Temple, passing through Guimard's elegant Art Nouveau entrance to daube swastikas on Le Marais' graceful Guimard synagogue.

He had travelled outside Paris: to the Vatican, where he was blessed by the Pope and inducted as a financial factotum; to Washington, where he'd conferred with the great and the right.

He'd reminisce about those journeys whenever Line 2 carried him through Stalingrad: Commies, the anti-Christ, they deserved everything that they'd got.

When Central America lurched towards Marxism he had ensured that donations to the church, from the poor of those countries, went to right-wing militias. The USA had paid compensation in dollars, millions of dollars, which were easily funnelled into grateful vaults.

May 1st is a national holiday, a socialist holiday, and the platform at Odéon heaved with gaiety. A whine above the crowd's heads and a gust of rank air announced the arrival of the train. A firm hand between his shoulder blades, and he met his fate. Amid the screams of the horrified, the assassin slipped away.

His obituary would say that he was a great man and a good Catholic. It would not mention that he was a thief. And no-one steals from Domini Canis: God's Dogs.

A Sign of Comfort—Sue St. John

It's Spring and the promise of new life. Sitting at her desk she looks out of the kitchen window past the daffodils and apple blossom, all she can see is a ball and an empty water bowl.

A week ago, they had made the right but difficult decision; a week of tears, feeling foolish for crying over a stupid dog. A part of the family, their routine, how empty life feels. The once yearned for lie-in now just spent staring at the bedroom ceiling.

'Tap, tap, tap.' She looks over to the French doors and sees a blue tit tapping at the windowpane. A brief smile flickers across her face then she returns to staring out into the garden.

She remembers how Benji would sit the other side of the doors waiting impatiently to be let in, his mucky paws smearing the glass as he jumped up demanding her attention. Something else to clean, to clear up. Her heavy heart not yet ready.

'Tap, tap, tap.' When they came back from their walks she liked to leave him outside while she made herself a coffee and prepared his breakfast.

'Tap, tap, tap.' She was dreading this morning. The David Austen Rose 'Sweet Dreams' standing in readiness by the border.

'Tap, tap, tap.' This little bird seems intent on disrupting her thoughts; she pops out of the back door to watch him.

He turns, his little wings fluttering fast to enable him to hover in the air. He stares at her for just a bit longer than a moment then flies away, a spirit free to dance in the sky.

Her phone rings, the call she's been waiting for. The vet's gentle voice on the other end of the line, 'Benji's back, we have his ashes, you can bring him home.'

Alarm—Polly Stretton

'You alright?'

Who's phoning at this hour?

'You OK?' It's Fliss. 'They told me, get to yours, 'cos I'm the primary key holder,' she says, 'house alarm…meet police there.'

The alarm had shrieked earlier, police arrived, hammered on the door, scanned the garden, grumbled off, 'Nothing wrong here.' And now, Fliss.

'I came. All dark. No police. I sat in the car 'cos someone might kill me,' she giggled. 'Waited. Nothing. Thought you must be OK. Came home. Tried your landline. No reply. Called your mobile, knew I wouldn't sleep without speaking to you. You alright?'

I know I'll never hear the end of this then feel ashamed, Fliss is my best friend. But something creeps in my middle. 'I'm sorry you came over for nothing,' I say, stomach clenched and not knowing why. 'Sorry you missed the police.'

'I was asleep. Had to find your keys,' she complains, 'not easy,' keys rattle, 'I got dressed,' she revs up, 'Scared to death. Could've been killed,' she sobs, 'kept wondering, what if they're all dead? What if robbers saw me, turned off the lights?'

'It's OK, Fliss,' I say, 'we're fine.' I put my slowness down to the hour, 'Have they called you before?'

'No,' she says—succinct for Fliss.

'Weird,' I say, 'we've had the alarm fourteen years. It's gone off before.'

'Why'd they phone me tonight, then?'

'Who phoned?'

'Your alarm company said meet the police…most insistent.'

'Where are you now, Fliss?' That creepy feeling's back. 'Who's your alarm with?'

'I don't have one,' says Fliss, 'and after this I won't! I'm just going in, I needed to talk—'

'Don't go in, Fliss. Call the police. They're in your house

or have been. Call the police!'

I hear her footsteps, the smash of glass and Fliss screaming, 'Nooooooo…'

Alternative Therapies—Helen Beckett

I throw my arms around the tree as if my life depends on it.

Carys had laughed, reaching up to the clouds as she'd swung back and forth. 'Let's go to the greenhouse now, Mummy.'

'I don't think there is one.' But I'd followed her anyway. A few brave blooms on the rose bushes were adding a final splash of autumnal colour to the dying borders.

Carys skipped ahead of me, stopping to point to a glass building that had, till then, been shielded by a small copse of trees.

'How did you know it was here?'

'I came here with Daddy and Jess.'

'Who's Jess?'

'She's my new friend.'

I'd not met her. I made a mental note to ask Iain about her when he returned home from Frankfurt.

I push my cheek into the rough bark, enjoying the jolt of pain as a jagged edge scratches my skin. I hug my tree harder, relishing its reliability, needing its constancy

We'd driven home down a street of elegant Georgian terraced houses.

'That's Jess's house,' Carys shouted. 'The one with the red door.'

I looked across and saw the cars parked on the road, clocking the black Mercedes with the personalised number plate. I pulled over.

'Are we going to call on Jess?' Carys leaned over her booster seat to undo her seat belt.

'No. Stay in the car,' I ordered, my voice sounding harsh and unnatural.

I walked up the steps and rang the bell, resisting the urge to kick the symmetrically-placed potted plants that stood on either side of the door. It was opened by a tall, dark-haired man whose face fell as he saw me.

'Hello, Iain,' I said, giving in to the urge to kick the perfect pots into a million pieces.

Bottled Up Emotions—Jan Baynham

Mam opens the buff-coloured telegram and, in silence, reads the words staring up at her. Her face blanches. Her whole body shakes. I rush to her side, but she brushes me away.

'I'm fine. We knew it was coming. He's been missing for months.'

I stifle a sob, tears burning.

My mother's talking again. 'It's no good getting all maudlin about it. It's happening to hundreds of other families every single day. Besides, I've got that posh dress of yours to finish, haven't I?'

How can she think of such things? She's just received confirmation of what we'd all been dreading. My brother, her eldest son, has been killed in action. How can I meet with the vicar for a wedding rehearsal with Frank? It isn't right but I know Mam. Even though her heart is shrinking inside her, she keeps it all buttoned up, getting my wedding gown done, just for me. All I want is to fling my arms around her and tell her to cry all the hurt and sorrow away.

Stoic, that's the word. Keeping a stiff upper lip. A 'life-has-to-go-on' attitude. Doesn't she now see everything in monochrome? Struggle to breathe? Feel physical pain from a heart split in two? All the time, my mother is busy. Her sewing box open on the table, she meticulously stitches the pinned hem of my dress. Fine stitches that won't show through the delicate parachute silk. The final touches to a garment made with love.

'You'd better get going, *cariad*.'

'But, Mam…'

'Now go,' she says. 'And don't stumble over them vows.'

She rises from the table and pushes me to the door.

Outside, the metallic grey sky reflects how I feel. As I reach the front gate, a piercing howl from inside the cottage shatters the silence.

Corners—Seraphim Bryant

I have a face tattoo. Yes, I'm that kind of girl. My father tried 'belt' discipline, and my mother would send me to the 'naughty spot' in the corner of the living room. Despite their efforts, I have and always will have a healthy disrespect for authority. Still, from the corner of the classroom and the lengthy detentions after home-time, I became a priest.

Oh yes, you read that right. It was not the church of God I loved; as previously stated, I'm not authority friendly. People were my addiction. I was in prison for a drug addiction related felony, and I was an alcoholic too; that's when I read about 'JESUS'. I liked the way that dude loved and lived, so I followed his game plan.

It may feel as though some of us have been relegated to the corners, but here's the thing: from the corners, I can see the whole room. I love the corners. I always have. It is where I will always choose to sit because I love outcasts, queers and girls who talk too loud. I love the humour that comes out of lives that have not been easy. I love sober drunks, single dads, sex workers and the guy who lost a leg in the war. I'm Nadia Bolz-Weber an ordained Lutheran Pastor. These are my people, and this is my faith.

Echoes of the Lark—Leena Batchelor

Shivering in the grimed scraps that passed as clothes, Mary crouched patiently, awaiting the final ebb of the tide. Orphaned at the tender age of four, Mary had learnt to survive alongside the mudlark gangs combing the banks running from Vauxhall Bridge to Blackwall.

Now fifteen, Mary was determined to avoid the trap of belonging to one of the slavering men that bought findings from her. A possibility had presented itself yesterday from a young scullery maid who bought a scrap of delicate blue ribbon carefully washed from the mud, a possibility with a clean bed and board, luxuries Mary could only dream of.

Shouts and calls echoed along the banks as the children sank into the dragging mud. The stench of human detritus and rotting waste made the air dense, almost palpable, and Mary felt herself gag as her hand closed on a decaying carcass. She morosely wiped her soiled hand on a scrap of skirt, and decided. She still had her looks and remained untouched by those who scanned her lithe body with piggy eyes. All she needed was a bath and an opportunity.

The call of a lark warned of Peelers approaching. Mary frantically pulled herself up the bank, seeking refuge in a sewer pipe peeping out from among the reeds. The warmth and darkness suffused into her weary bones, inviting her to close her eyes. Welcoming a brief respite before encroaching tides forced her to leave the murky sanctuary, Mary closed her eyes.

Contented with her efforts, Anna wiped her brushes and placed them alongside the fresh canvas sitting pertly on its easel. Stretching, curiously watching the shifting mist rolling in and flowing into a disused sewer pipe rusting in the reeds beneath her feet, the name 'Mary' echoed in her ears.

Fallen by the Trackside—Lisa Johnston

She'd noticed him on the escalator. Rain coat, dark suit and haircut that would cost her a month's wages. His right foot in polished brogue tapped the metal step. A woman's backpack shifted to reveal his fingernails testing the hard rubber of the handrail whilst people snaked onto the platform. His hands were large, clean, the marble of his wrist bone showed at the white cuff of his shirt. She ran possibilities of lives he might lead whilst descending into the caverns of the station. Turning left onto the platform; his striking, elegant face of indeterminate age drew looks from other commuters awaiting the homeward crush. She followed to the far end of the platform; in between shoppers with branded bags, laughing about expensive lunches and purchases, teenagers in school uniforms, faces of workers in varying degrees of despondency until stopping, too far from the signage to know the destination of incoming trains. He tested the paint of the yellow line as if he wanted to rub it out, put his bag down like a small dog at heal then walked forward to test if it would sit and stay.

A deep rumble and commuters instinctively moved wavelike across the platform to greet the sea wall of closed carriage doors. She walked quickly behind him as she saw his right foot leave the yellow line and slide over the grey kerb. The steel gleam of headlights as one brogue disappeared. With two handfuls of raincoat she sat down heavily on the platform, counter-levering his body weight to join her, one behind the other, as if they were in an 80s disco doing the moves to 'Oops upside your head'.

'I think I lost my shoe,' he said wiggling the toes of his right foot in a surprisingly multi-coloured striped sock.

Good Morning Midnight—Leena Batchelor

The deadly-sharp edge of the pick glanced off the wall and slipped from her cold hands; she was tired, physically and emotionally wrung-out. The only company of the last few hours the insistent whack-whack of the pick against the ice-wall.

The humming machines which maintained the cycles of day and night had cried to the dark recesses of her mind; they were in pain, no longer able to support the complex subterranean infrastructure. No one remembered who had built these monoliths; their power rumoured to come from an energy source above the surface. But no one was left who remembered what the surface looked like since humanity had been consigned to the depths to escape the virus.

Flexing and blowing upon her fingers to renew vitality, she picked up the heavy wooden-handled pick. Legends talked of wood coming from trees upon the surface, a living and beautiful place, so different to the colourless expanses their current existence offered. She did not know if the surface had maintained this vitality, yet held hope of a freedom from the confines of their current claustrophobic life.

A final swing splintered the handle, cracking the ice beneath. A deep resonance vibrated through her mind, while lights flickered and the low thrum of machines was replaced with a sharp snap as a switch revealed itself. Pulling herself upright upon shaking legs, her trembling fingers reached out…

A small console beneath her hand lit up with four short statements:

Viral Rescue Station Alpha.
All levels sealed.
Countdown initiated.

As if in trepidation, the wall grew brighter, becoming increasingly translucent as time ticked by, each minute becoming unmistakably brighter, until finally an opening dissolved…

Her eyes took in the brightness as she stepped forward and

welcomed the dawn. Midnight had become the hour of her freedom.

Grandad's Sycamore Tree—Joy Ryland

Archie left the laughter behind him and walked out to the patio in the warm July sunshine. Feeling unbearably hot in his best suit, he stood in the relative quiet of the garden staring down at the tall sycamore. His father followed him out.

'Your gramps would have enjoyed this. He loved a good knees-up, although he would have hated having to dress up in this heat. He was always more at home in his shorts and sandals.'

'I was thinking about all the good times we've had in this house. Every year on my birthday, right up to the day I went away to uni, Gramps marked my height on that tree trunk. I miss him so much.'

'Gramps and I had a chat a few weeks ago. He felt his time was running out and he came to a decision. He's left the house to you and Beth. He knew you loved the place and he really wanted to keep it in the family. He said you would need the space, with the baby on the way.'

'How did he know Beth was pregnant? We only found out last week.'

'You know what Gramps was like he always seemed to have sixth sense.'

They walked over the manicured lawn down to the sycamore. Looking round the tree at all the family names and dates, Archie couldn't believe what he saw. Carved on the trunk underneath his and Beth's names, was a gap, then a date. Opened mouthed he looked at his father.

'That's for your son's name when you've chosen it.'

'We've already decided. If it's a boy he'll be called Jack, after Gramps.'

'Let's hope he's predicted the correct date.'

'Have you ever known Gramps to be wrong?'

Guilty Secrets—Jan Baynham

Sinister, ominous shadows lurk around the cemetery. Crows gather on the leafless branches of trees lining the pathway that led to a gaping hole in the ground. A *murder* of crows, particularly fitting for the occasion, as if to bear witness to his interment. The verdict was self-defence, but we all know what really happened to Lucy. Taking his own life was proof he couldn't live without her, *they* said. Proof of a guilty secret more like. Perhaps he had a conscience after all.

'Dust to dust, ashes to ashes.'

The vicar's words bring me back to earth with a bump.

With sombre expressions, coal-black attire, silent tears, mourners watch as he's lowered into the earth. His sister reads a poem. *I am not dead…* Hearing those words, a shiver fizzles through my whole body. Please God that he is. Let it be over. Finally.

Lucy's body lying mutilated and ravaged in the mortuary could so easily have been me. I should have spoken out but chose to stay silent. Because of me, her son has no mother, her parents no daughter. I clench my fists, my nails digging into my palms.

The brittle sound of the cawing crows shatters the still air. I want to scream too. Maybe he couldn't live with the guilt that he'd got away with it. Lucy would never have attacked him first. And yet still I said nothing. Why? I ask myself that every day.

'Oh, Sophie. Thank you for coming. You will come back to the house, won't you?'

Guilt washes over me again as his mother's eyes fill with tears. She doesn't know why I really came.

'No. I must get back. But thank you.'

I look up as the black crows disperse, flying high into the steel grey sky. He's gone.

High Rise—Polly Caley

We are the stories we tell ourselves—next slide, please—but what if we've lost the plot?

Moments before, I was on a park bench contemplating sesame seeds, the burger in my hand suddenly unappetising, my iPhone tossed aside after digesting the news. Now I'm on the ledge of lost hope, feeling locked down to the point of wanting to bolt free, off the edge.

I rose up here with the 'R' rate, needing to take the air, out of despair. In my reality 'R' might be Relationship failures, Race-related injustice, maybe just a run of 'Rotten luck', as the well-meaning old girl at flat 104 observes. All of them endemic—all of them ending me.

If I become a sad statistic, which cause will the effect be pinned on in the data? Right now, I'd ditch all of the science for winged angels to catch me when I step off, returning me to a lighter feeling.

I look at my trainers as I shuffle along. A tiny scrap of dead leaf flutters momentarily, unpeels itself from my shoe and departs, gliding effortlessly down, mockingly.

Just as I wonder if I'll fail at this too, I see I'm not alone up here. She was here first, somehow found her way on to this ledge. Two fearful eyes meet mine and I am alert to the voice of the universe: it's not all about me. She's shaking, she's broken. She can't speak but it's clear I'm needed.

I'm so careful in my approach and I tuck my hands around her gently. I coo at her reassuringly. I place her snugly in my inside jacket pocket, next to my heart. Some may call her a sky rat, but I say angel and I climb down in search of sesame seeds for her.

It's Probably Your Clutch—Hedy Lewis

'I can't quite put my finger on it,' Chardonnay said, for the fourth time in as many minutes. I didn't look up. This level of angst rolled around every Wednesday night. 'I just, I'm just not right. Something's wrong.'

Don't worry, she didn't mean her health, physical or otherwise. She meant her outfit. Now, I'm not dumbing that down, Wednesday night was very important to her, but I'd shared a house with Chardonnay for four years, you become immune to the drama after a while.

'Have you tried changing your outfit completely?' I asked, that usually fixed it.

'Twice.' Came the reply. 'Oh, it's nearly nine, I've got to go, everyone will be wondering where I am.' Everyone being the Wednesday night regulars at the Admiral Rodney, the local pub, you know, the one with the reputation that kept the football hooligans away.

'What about your shoes? Maybe it's your shoes?'

'But I love them,' she sighed, running a finger over the red sequinned stilettos.

I gave in and looked up. Took in the six-inch heels, the figure-hugging dress, the ocean of hair, a completely different colour to what it had been last week. 'It's probably your clutch,' I said at last, pointing to her tiny handbag, just the right size for notes and lipstick.

Chardonnay beamed and ran upstairs.

She brought down three glittery options, and together we chose just the right one. With a cherry red specimen selected, she squealed in triumph, kissed my forehead and exited exuberantly through the door. She wouldn't be back until I was in bed, so I wouldn't see Chardonnay for another week.

Tomorrow she'd be Dave. Safe, dependable Dave. Who worked in accounts and drove a beige Volvo, and lived his life waiting for Wednesday night at the Admiral Rodney.

Just Another Day at School—
John (Mogs) Morris

He was leaning back on the hood of his patrol car sipping coffee when the call came over the radio, 'All units; shots reported at the high-school.'

Calculating he'd be there quicker on foot, he dashed to the alley, drawing his weapon and letting coffee splatter across the sidewalk.

At the gate there were screaming kids running in all directions. He saw the first body slumped against the main door, blood still trickling from two holes in the janitor's chest.

'We have casualties,' he said into his radio. There was a shot. 'Shooter still active, I'm going in.' He didn't even hear the girl on dispatch tell him to wait for backup.

There were three more bangs, some screams, another four, then silence. As he edged down the corridor. Two more shots, sounding closer now. Turning a corner. More bodies, students this time. A few paces more and he peered into a classroom. The smell of cordite strong now. A pretty blond girl in her mid-teens lay slumped against a wall, her summer dress soaked in blood.

'Police, drop your weapon,' he shouted, gun aimed at the back of a dark figure.

The man slowly turned, lowering his semi-automatic and dropping it to the floor as their eyes met.

'Marty!?'

'Dad?' the boy replied. How strange that during the weeks of fantasising about this day he'd never considered this possibility.

As uniformed figures entered the school there was a single shot from somewhere down the corridor.

Radios crackled into life. A cold, calm voice said, 'Assailant neutralised.'

Keith, Alberta, and the Posse—Safia Sawal

Keith could see Alberta sitting up on the red rocks sipping single malt from a flask; it's a short climb and the posse follow him in a uniform line. Regular walkers in the valley smile acknowledgement at the tall man in his faded denim, faithfully followed by his posse of five tiny Heinz 57's. His long limbs flop down onto the rock and the posse hurtle down the bank to play in the valley below, while Keith watches the buzzard's swoop.

'Where shall we go today, Alberta, on the wings of our buzzards?'

Keith closes his eyes, they're both on the yacht: blue skies, blue sea, the Mediterranean. He soaks up the warmth and enjoys the breeze on his face. The posse are back, the sun low behind the trees; he shivers and makes his way home.

The posse find Alberta, asleep, they all have their own place on the bed to snuggle in with her.

Keith tells Alberta where he flew with the buzzards today. They've always flown together; he asks her, 'Which life is your favourite?'

'This life,' she says, 'is our best life, here in the valley with the posse and the buzzards.'

Keith watches his posse chasing each other while the buzzard's swoop. He closes his eyes and gazes towards the Statue of Liberty, Alberta walking by his side, it's night and there's a full moon. He lives this American life fleetingly, before the posse run around him, scrabbling at his back, time for dinner.

The house is so quiet now, the posse sleep on the bed, in their own places. Keith slips in and out of his lives less and less, but every day he watches the posse play, the buzzard's swoop and sips his single malt with Alberta.

Labyrinthine Sewers—Jacquie Gillespie

Theo, sweating under his high vis jacket and waders arrived at the prearranged place. His chest ached; retirement definitely beckoned.

He expected the apprentice to be waiting for him above ground. He was going to show him 'the ropes'. Where was the boy? Maybe he had gone ahead, but the manhole cover was still in place. He would have to go down on his own. He hated it down there. There was something eerie about it. He was happier when someone was with him.

'Hello.' He called into the darkness. Someone snorted. His apprentice *had* gone down ahead of him. 'He must be keen,' he thought.

'You really should have waited for me.'

There was no reply. He hurried past the figure, who moved deeper into the shadows.

It was hot and the stench, as he walked along the tunnel, took his breath away. He'd get used to it after a while he knew. The figure behind him must have a cold, as usually apprentices complained about the smell. Small creatures scampered over their feet on the narrow ledge above the dark underground river.

'Mind your step, it's slippery on this bit.'

The figure grunted and followed him.

Ahead of them, picked out in the torch light, was a large whiteish grey object blocking the tunnel, a fat berg.

'We'll have to break it up,' Theo said, climbing slowly down into the water.

The figure clothed in shadow remained silent and still.

Eventually, Theo finished stacking the slippery glutinous lumps in a pile. Above him a muscular arm reached down and effortlessly set him back up on the ledge. Standing stiffly, Theo brushed himself down.

Then he looked up and for the first time he saw the creature's face and holding his chest he gasped…

Life, Explained by Death—Jamie D Stacey

Whatever way you look at it, it's a gravestone.

I know I've given up when I take to the Sunday morning walk at the cemetery. I've given up on God and wander the winter corridors behind His church. How many steps behind me, how many ahead? Do I care? I look to the graves, this drooping stone, as after a stroke.

Near the entrance I walk past the many Joneses and Llewellyns. Past a mound of dirt, I come across a Larkin; like the one at school who beat me like a slab of wet meat and I kept shut.

Past the angel statue thick in myrtle green moss, there are autumn leaves that fall like fat tears down the Jacobs and Smiths. Shy of 17, I never did ask Amy out, only watched as she disappeared into someone else's night.

I walk on. A Cavalli; I never did get selected for the rugby team at Brynteg. A Pettigrew, a Peter, and under the hush of trees, a Dragon; I never did get that promotion at the DVLA. My feet sink and squelch in yesterday's rain, until I reach the summit where tomorrow's sun shines like flecks of gold, only to disappear with the gang of clouds plotting above. End of the path and there are no more graves, no more names; no one here who won the lottery either.

Because who in this cemetery became more than just a name caught between life and death?

I hear the church bells ring against my back. I make to leave only to stumble across a gravestone I don't recognise. A new stone, winter primrose whispering: *Olivia (2021-2021).* The bells ring inside. I read again, hold the name until it blurs in my eyes, and then I remember everything else…

I have lived.

Locked Down Hitman's Blues—Martin Driscoll

I think I have suffered during Covid more than anyone else I know; as soon as social distancing kicked in that made my work as an 'up close and personal' assassin nigh on impossible.

I'm not one of those cold, dispassionate, take 'em out with a long range high velocity sniper sight malarkey, there's no skillset in that, any Call of Duty watching nerk could do THAT. I worked hard at making the connections with my 'mark', tracking, surveillance, knowing their routines and lifestyle, god, I got closer than their loved ones without them even knowing…

And now, keep two metres apart: how does putting a lightning strike blade work now?

And don't start me off with masks!

I must be the only outlaw NOT wearing a mask. I have terrible asthma and my contact lenses always steam up with a mask so that's no go, too young to get the jab (another one of MY tricks by the way) and can't exactly ask the doctors for an exclusion note to wave at victims.

So of course, no contracts means no income. I can't exactly apply for the Government's self-employed SEISSE grant and we are not exactly a unionized group of workers but I AM a freelance worker with rights. Try telling that to organized crime, more like DIS-organized crime during all this let me tell you…

So in essence, I've been given the bullet—made redundant by Covid, kind of apt I suppose.

Lovers Long Gone—Claire Llewellyn

Squeak…Squeak…Squeak…

That familiar sound from the apartment above, yet again disturbs my fitful sleep. It was three in the morning for heaven's sake; some of us had to get up in a few hours and bleed for 'the man' in order to keep this thin ceiling above their heads! Cosy couples would say I was just bitter, been single too long. Nevertheless, I was quite content in my miserable solitude. I would be more content of course, if I could get a decent night's kip!

I tried to complain to the management on many occasions, only to be dismissed as neurotic! The other tenants whispered behind my back, avoiding eye contact. Once I knocked on the door of said apartment, hearing a low giggling and shuffling as I stood waiting to deliver my appeal. I never saw the occupants. Who were they? Why was everyone so evasive? I had to have some resolution; I could not go on like this.

The next evening I plotted and waited for the inconsiderate pair to commence their ritual lovemaking. I quietly proceeded to the offending apartment, crowbar and bucket of cold water in hand. I forced the door and braced myself. Ready to cool the coital couple, I entered the bedroom…the room was empty!

Mature—Kate Jones

The cheddar was tired of the youngsters' antics, the cherry tomatoes were the worst, rolling around the salad drawer in fits of giggles. In his more senior years Cheddar was feeling his age, stuck in the door he felt irritated by being called Ched by the spring onions and he was far too mature to behave like the strawberries constantly hugging each other. It was as if they had something to prove. 'Oh, darling, kiss kiss.'

The plastic stuff stayed around longer; they had a chat with Cheddar when the kids were asleep. They all knew the kids wouldn't last long, so tolerated them and their jollities. They hoped they would be taken in their prime and not left to get sick; it was sad to see such a demise and quite frankly rather smelly.

Cheddar's closest friends were the eggs at the other end of the shelf. They were always fed up with the cold and wanted to be outside in the kitchen. Eggs should be at room temperature they kept complaining. Not until they were released and beaten did they see the light of day. Cheddar found this extra sad as he knew he'd have to supply some body parts to contribute to the beating.

Occasionally, next to the milk, a plastic jug would appear full of lemons, limes and water. Water is superior to all the other food stuffs; it is the only one which is essential and the only one with no calories. This made it very popular at certain times but quite often ignored when the chocolate was living next door, especially the dark stuff constantly doing the Samba.

It was shopping day, a new cheese in town. Cheddar accepted his fate and was gone, into the darkness.

Mine—Polly Stretton

It was her house, not his. How dare he threaten to take it off her? What had he contributed? Nothing. That's what. Nothing. Barbara emptied drawers into black bags and threw them down to the pavement.

He turned up later. 'Barb, let me in, I need to talk to you, we need to talk. Barb,' his mouth was to the letterbox, 'let me in. Think of the neighbours.'

'You think of the neighbours.'

'Barb, let me in.'

'Never. I know what you are. I can't live with someone who's threatened me. Take my house away? I don't think so! You've only been here five minutes. Besides, it's my house, not yours, and possession is nine-tenths of the law.'

'Come down the pub later, at least talk to me there.'

She went, she listened, she laughed out loud; she walked home giggling to herself. It was her house, not his.

Moving On—Susan Howe

You know he's lying, of course. Just like all the other times he hasn't come home and then given some lame excuse about the car not starting or having had too much to drink. Actually, that's the one you did believe.

He knows that you know he's lying, yet he still does it, as if it's a ritual you are obliged to perform in order to move on. Does he think he's somehow protecting you? Because it doesn't feel like it.

'Do you want some breakfast?' you ask, to show him you don't bear grudges.

'No thanks,' he says. 'I need a shower.'

I'll bet you do, you refrain from saying aloud. You don't want a row. Following him upstairs, you collect his clothes for the wash.

Twenty minutes later he comes down, his cheeks flushed and hair tousled. You catch your breath. He's so handsome, it's no wonder women fancy him.

'Coffee?' You reach for the machine.

'In a minute,' he says. 'First I've got something to tell you.'

You stiffen. Your scalp prickles.

He sits at the table and gestures you towards the chair opposite. Shivering slightly, you pull your cardigan closer round yourself and sit.

He looks you square in the eye and takes a deep breath.

'I've met someone special and we want to move in together,' he says, all in a rush.

There's a loud buzzing in your head and your sight blurs. Bile rises in your throat and you sway in your seat. He puts out a hand to catch you.

'Are you alright, Mum?' he says, his face the picture of concern.

You blink, swallow and try to sit up straight.

'Yes, of course I am,' you manage.

But this time you both know which one of you is lying.

Next Left for Unbelievable Attractions—James Mason

If you had followed the instructions on the hand painted sign and, indicating, turned your car down the pinched little lane that bumped and rattled for a country mile between the dark shadows of the trees, you would have found us waiting: the trail bursting out of the undergrowth onto a wide, unkempt lawn (showing off a rusty swing set and a derelict Austin 8 that was busy melting back into the earth), at the end of which, its slate roof slumped and windows clouded with cataracts of dust, was the Museum of Unusual Things.

You might have asked aloud if this was it? Perhaps started to turn your car. Except, of course, it would have been too late. We would have been out at once—the curator who, in his starched collar, always looked as strange and formal as a taxidermied frog, and me with my high shoulder and gong farmer's limp. It was only two rooms, with warped floorboards and the smell of rising damp. You would walk around, aloof, embarrassed; a trifle confused as to what you were doing there.

'Look, here,' the curator would croak and hold each treasure up: a unicorn's hoof, one scale from the basilisk, the cockatrice wattle donated by M. Perkis. Rarer still: a lock of Lamia's hair; a nugget of rock mined by gnomes. Finally, Puck's signature on a postcard; on the front a faded daguerreotype of, we think, Rhyl.

If you, on a whim, decide to visit again, to risk your car and jolt back down the path, you'll only find a clearing in a wood, at the end of which is a rectangle of yellow grass and some blacken timbers still hugging the last wispy scents of smoke. We have moved on, of course, this being a rational age.

Perspective—Safia Sawal

It started with eggs, images of caged and cramped birds and horrendous stories of beak trimming. Then Jess read a book on salmon farming in Scotland and watched a television programme about a pig farm. She told her mum she was going to be a vegan and Mum thought, that'll be fine, lots of people don't eat animal foods for lots of different reasons and they all survive and some feel much better for it, much healthier.

Jess got caught up in her research. She was reading as much as she could, accessing social media sites, blogs and articles coming at her from all directions. She watched videos and documentaries and forgot about her lectures. She'd made no friends, so no one was there to notice. She messaged her mum: 'all good,' 'fine here,' 'speak soon'. Mum messaged back with tips and recipes for being a vegan.

Jess listened to a podcast telling her that soya is bad for the environment and has been implicated in thyroid problems. She read that avocados are an unethical fruit, also bad for the environment, the liver, and the bees, so avocados are not a vegan food. She watched a film about non-stick pans and threw out all her cookware. Then she read about water and her brain only registered lead, hormones and microplastics.

Jess didn't message her mum. The paramedics made it in time.

Her nostrils twitched and saliva formed at the corners of her mouth, the smell of garlic and ginger hung in the air, she could hear a whispered conversation, her eyes flickered open and Mum and Dad sprung into domestic action, smiles, hugs, and soup. Home grown, homemade, Jess was hungry now, best vegetable soup ever.

Placating the Masses—Roz Levens

'More complaints, Christian.'

'Oh for God's sake, what do they want, blood?'

'Probably.'

Christian Dagger looked at the sheaf of emails the Fat Controller was offering. It's no fun being a Reality TV scheduler these days, he thought. Lockdown's seen to that.

'We can't do any filming that comes within two metres. We can't show hugging and kissing. We need hectares of Perspex screening, and yet the great viewing public want reality as they remember it, before the Great Plague.' He sighed. 'I really don't know what we can do.'

'Peleton's trending.'

'The Tour de France? Are they still running that?'

'It's not that any more. That fitness lot copyrighted the word. Now it's people in London yelling at you remotely while you exercise in your own home.'

'Would people watch that?'

'Humiliation's always popular.'

'True.' He jotted a note in his phone. 'What else?'

'That pottery thing with the judge that cries.'

'Oh yes, true. I've watched that myself. Just to see if he cries, of course. Not the pottery.'

'Of course.'

'What about antiques?'

'No. Aunty Beeb's got the monopoly on that one.'

'We could do something new—make people think the stuff in their kitchen cupboards and garden sheds is trendy and valuable—you know, old Flymos, and Kitchen Devil knives, that sort of thing.'

Christian considered his list, his head on one side. 'Could we combine the three?'

'What? How?'

'Dunno. Like a triathlon, somehow. They have to make something, race to a junk shop with it and persuade the shop owner to swap it for a "new" antique.' He made inverted commas in the air around the word 'new'.

'Brilliant. What do we call it?'

There was a moment of intense silence. Christian smiled like a wolf.

'Throw Up, It's Worth It?'

Pork—Fritz Cavelle

My family's position in the bedrock of English aristocracy had been established by an ancestor who was rewarded for his involvement in the Crusades, the Third I think.

He had been an illiterate pig farmer in Aquitaine who, fired with religious fervour and porcine indignation, had marched to the Cross armed with a sackful of piglets. On gaining the Holy Land there remained a breeding drove of several sows and one legless boar. He enamoured himself to the Hospitaliers by providing pork products much to the chagrin of the Templars, Moslems and Jews.

He gained eminence as a combatant; whilst knights and sergeants were expected to exhibit fighting prowess, the common pilgrims were considered little more than ballast to occupy Muslim blades. This man however could wield knives and was unaffected by the spillage of blood. He proved himself by slitting the throats of captives at Acre, wading through their blood as he dispatched them with a single stroke.

He stood witness to the Lionheart's withdrawal at Jerusalem's walls and later to his incarceration by the Holy Roman Emperor. It is said that he carried messages as part of the negotiations to ransom the King and for that was rewarded with a fief in the country that Richard most despised: England.

And now, a thousand years later, I feel that I have a special right to be honoured. After all, hadn't my interest-free loan to the Chairman enabled him to purchase his bijou flatette in Knightsbridge? And the PM, as vacuous and self-serving a narcissist as he is, surely couldn't forget the influential soirees that I threw on his behalf at my country pile? So, in this reshuffle, I expect a position of influence, in the Min of Ag or even the Treasury; whichever has the biggest barrel of pork.

Sex and Death—James Mason

In later years, the Captain decided it must have been a hoax. What else could it be? The Captain, who was then in the Revolutionary Guard, was driving the thirty miles between his wife and his mistress. The day was burned white and the Jeep's engine sounded lonely and brazen. The noise annoyed him. He had no wish to be shot to pieces on an isolated road with only cicadas to witness.

He gunned his vehicle up a sandy mesa and saw two women lounging under a lime tree. At first, he assumed they might be the wives of two men he had recently executed, but these women were unlikely to consort with bandits, being beautifully attired in silk dresses and wide-brimmed hats. He called out that this was a strange place for a picnic!

Yes, the women agreed, but he should come join them.

The air under the lime tree was so cool that the Captain shivered. Not wanting to be ungallant, he pretended not to. The women sat on a rug and regarded him with eyes hidden by the brims of their sunhats.

What is it you want? asked one. The Captain felt foolish, after all there were lots of things.

Figs, he said, for, at that moment, he decided what he was most was hungry.

One of the women reached up and plucked two ripe, purple figs from the lime tree.

What do I do with them? the Captain asked. It was a child's question. The figs looked too perfect to eat.

He squirmed under the women's gaze, even though they were only women and he a full Captain in the Revolutionary Guard.

Finally, one replied: Captain, may you have a lifetime to answer.

Even years later, the Captain worried he had not understood the question.

The Biography—Kevin Brooke

Sometimes, I'd hear the rattle of the letter box. Other times, it was the rap of his fingers against the window pane. He'd drift into the cottage, his outline familiar, but scarcely visible. He was never any trouble and if he'd stayed longer, I would have been grateful.

I'd been spending too much time alone, writing the biography of a tormented life. The task had consumed me entirely and the opportunity to speak to this man and explain the intricacies of the manuscript offered me comfort.

Especially tonight.

'I've finished,' I told him. 'My life's work is complete.'

As the church clock chimed its mournful beat, I sensed the glimpse of a smile as he looked in my direction and mouthed, 'Goodbye.'

For the first time since we'd met, this ghost of a man had offered me contact and I followed him as he drifted out of the front door. In the bitter cold of moonlight, the fog lingered in the fields, its tendrils creeping through the trees and I tightened the collar of my jacket. The spirit headed along the pathway and when he reached the churchyard, he disappeared.

The fog thickened and smothered the light of the moon. I retraced my steps and when I arrived home, an increasing wind rattled the letter box to heighten a feeling of déjà vu. I glanced through the window to see the ghost of a man in my chair. His outline familiar, I rapped my fingers on the glass.

I went inside the cottage and exhaled deeply as I recognized both the man and the faded manuscript in his hand. I'd always believed that the effort of writing the biography would kill me. Now it was true. As the church bells chimed, I smiled, mouthed, 'Goodbye,' and drifted into the mist.

The Flowers are Dying, Mother—
Claire Llewellyn

'Thank you, sweetheart. They're perfect,' Mother croaked. Her thin smile attempted to hide her pain. Pain no one should wish upon another. Yet this pain was a gift!—a parting gift from my father. A man of simple pleasures, never excessive but hooked just the same. A revolting habit, years in the making and then breaking of the man. It seeped through his pores, stained his teeth and fingernails, fouled his breath, hair and clothing. It turned our living room into a teacher's lounge; turned my father into a husk…and Mother took it all in.

'Happy Anniversary.' I choked back tears as I lightly kissed her clammy forehead. Her frail hand reached out for mine. There was only love in her eyes. I sat beside her bed, young hand in old. Her strength ebbing. Strength that had built a home, a family. Strength that had healed my scraped knees and broken heart. Though her physical vigour was diminishing, her emotional fortitude was as stout as ever, and her love for the man who sealed her fate…unrelenting.

It had been one week since Mother joined Father once again on their special day. Every day I would visit her room and look at the flowers, (red roses with baby's-breath, her favourite). I would sit in her chair, reminiscing with a smile, all the while looking at the petals as they aged. This was my grieving process. As the petals dropped, I let go a little, until there were no more petals…and no more Mother.

The Gift of an Orange—Fritz Cavelle

My parents were communists. My father made shoes; my mother ran a bistro, both from the same premises. Some people came for wine and bought clogs. Some, looking for galoshes, took cider.

When the Germans came, it fell on the shoulders of my father to choose honest men and form a cadre of the Resistance, to make life as uncomfortable for the invaders as they could.

Two German soldiers, billeted in the town, frequented the bar even though they had been warned by the local gossip that we were communists.

On a September evening, just before curfew, my father and two friends were stopped at the edge of the town whilst returning from delivering bread to a nearby village. The leader of the patrol searched the three men and found a pistol hidden in my father's waistband. He did no more than pull it from my father's shirt and then use it to shoot him in the liver. He took days to die.

Despite what had happened, the two soldiers continued to drink in the bistro. My mother said, 'They are just men.'

In late December they came and drank well. That night they told my mother that they didn't want this, that they were both from communist families, that they had been conscripted, that they had children too.

They called me to them and gave me an orange. An orange. At four years old I had never seen one. These giants with ice-blue eyes had reached into the sky and handed me a sweet piece of the sun. It is my clearest memory of the war.

Later that evening they told us that this was the last time that we would see them, for the following morning they were to leave for the Eastern Front; to fight the communists.

The Investment—Kevin Brooke

Albert placed the keys on the table. They belonged to the house in which he'd raised his children, then comforted his dying partner, Annie, in her final few months. It was a place that meant everything, almost too much, and this was the reason he'd decided to move on.

'You've been done,' his brother said, when Albert showed him the contract. 'Zongo is a thief.'

'No,' Albert replied. 'He is a man of his word. You'll see.'

They'd corresponded via email, spoken on the phone and arranged to meet once the deal was finalised.

'The investment is free of risk and 100 percent guarantee,' Zongo confirmed. 'As well as a magnificent 40% of the business, you'll be helping the poor, motherless babies in the world.'

It was the legacy Albert craved, particularly as Zongo confirmed he'd be flown to a recently discovered island named Annie in memory of his wife. The only stipulation was that Albert should act quickly and when the sale of the house stalled, Zongo forced it through.

'It is part of the service,' Zongo confirmed, but then came the silence.

Albert's repeated calls were ignored and instead of being kept informed at every turn as promised, he heard nothing. Until the confirmation of eviction. Disowned by his brother and the rest of his family, Albert had nowhere to go. Without a backward glance at the house, he closed the front door behind him and turned towards the road in which a black limousine was parked. Convinced it belonged to the new owners of his house, he bowed his head as the tears welled in his eyes.

'Mr Albert,' a voice said. 'Your private jet is waiting for you.'

'Zongo?'

'I'm sorry for my quietness,' he replied. 'The investment is complete and everything is arranged as agreed.'

The Love Vaccine—Mark Kilburn

As Thomas stood in the queue outside his local health centre waiting for his vaccine shot a young man ran up to him. 'Don't do it,' he said. 'It's all lies. The government wants to control your brain.'

He pushed a crumpled leaflet into Thomas' hand then moved along the line before two burly security guards appeared. After a struggle and a lot of shouting the young man was escorted to a waiting police van.

Thomas unfurled the leaflet. Since the announcement that a Love vaccine had been developed a fierce debate had raged across the world. Those in favour said the vaccine would dispel anger and hatred, leading to a more peaceful and tolerant world. Those against said it was abnormal to eradicate natural human emotion—a trick, dreamt up by totalitarian governments who wanted to enslave the human race.

The woman in front of Thomas turned and said: 'You look as though you're having second thoughts.'

Thomas sighed. 'Suddenly, the Love vaccine sounds kind of scary.'

'Anger and hatred are contagious,' the woman said, 'a disease, a plague. Surely a world without conflict and war is worth fighting for? The Love vaccine is humankind's only chance.'

He nodded, yet he still had many doubts. Only last week a group of national leaders had publicly been given the vaccine. Even so, their detractors claimed the phials had been filled with an ineffective substitute.

'What should I do?' said Thomas.

The woman took his hand. 'My son spent his life promoting the cause of love but sadly died before the vaccine's development. Please, do it for his sake if nothing else.'

Thomas glanced at the leaflet. 'Protect Your Freedom to Hate!' was the headline. He screwed the paper into a ball, moved forward in the queue.

The Not-So Green Man—Mark Kilburn

Spring arrived and on the village green an old man stood beneath the bower of a tree, admiring the sweet new leaves.

'Why's he standing there?' I asked. 'A meeting? A secret rendezvous?'

'Who knows?' came the answer.

He was broad, this man, and looked well-travelled. Bearded, with long wiry hair, he wore a greatcoat that had seen better days. He paced to and fro as if tormented by loss—haunted, perhaps, by something deep in his past.

Spring turned to Summer. Summer turned to Autumn. Winter caught her breath. Still he waited. Dead leaves swirled around him, coveting the north wind's embrace. Yet the old man remained.

'Doesn't he get cold?' I said. 'Where does he sleep?'

'He sleeps beneath the tree,' came the answer, 'with one eye open. And as he sleeps the children lay food beneath the branches. They call him the Not-So Green Man.'

Soon the branches of the tree were frosted with ice. He blew into cupped hands, cheeks red as the Christmas berry, shoes sodden, his coat in rags, pockets filled with dead, brittle seed.

One night I saw his silhouette. The moon and its canopy of stars illuminated his face. The tree had become a Not-So Green Man.

At last, Spring arrived—shook her dusty curtains in the sun. The tree sparkled with tender green buds. The villagers sang, danced—washed their faces in new light. 'Now we can feast,' they said, 'eat and drink our fill.'

A year has passed by and I have learned many things. I wish, now, I had spoken with the Not-So Green Man. Today I'll lay a wreath in his memory, sit for a while beneath the bower of the tree.

The Not-So Green Man was waiting for me.

The Snorting Rhinoceros—Kevin Brooke

'Oh my,' the captain said, as the opposition streamed through the five-bar gate.

'Oh my, what?' I asked.

'It's Johnson.'

The banter in the dressing room ceased. Eyes widened. Assured expressions withered. With the season about to start, news spread of a terrifying fast bowler who was rumoured to leave a trail of broken bones in his path.

Ten minutes later, the captain returned to the dressing room and delivered the news I was dreading. 'We're batting.'

'Is it definitely my turn to open?' I asked.

My teammates leaned forward and shouted a single word in aggressive unison.

'Yes!'

Everyone hated opening. To ensure fairness, we'd decided to rotate the batting order and I'd already shirked the responsibility a few times. I'd also upset the captain with the occasional practical joke, and I could tell he wanted revenge.

'Try not to die, Peters,' he said, helpfully.

My heart racing, I signed the mark of the cross as I walked to the wicket. The angry expressions on the opposition's faces reminded me of the trick I'd played on them at the recent barbeque. How was I to know they'd eat the dodgy, half-cooked burgers and end up in hospital?

'Play,' said the umpire.

With the image of raw meat ingrained in my mind, I looked up to see Johnson charging in like a snorting rhinoceros. His teeth bared, he reached the stumps and let go. My shoulders tightened, my hands began to tremble, but instead of the ferocious rocket I was expecting, the ball looped from Johnson's hand. It was ridiculously slow, and I swished my bat one way, then the other, lost my balance and fell onto the stumps.

'This time, Peters, the joke's on you,' Johnson said, as I picked myself up and walked, red-faced, towards my sniggering teammates.

The Truth About Horoscopes—Roz Levens

In faith, a difference of opinion that leads to a parting of the ways is known as a schism. In families, that's a rift.

Curiously, the root for both schism and rift is 'cleft'.

Father Patrick Mulvaney was a pillar of the church. He had a twinkle in his eye, glorious waves in his snow-white hair and a cleft to rival Kirk Douglas's in his chin. He rattled his newspaper angrily at his housekeeper.

'Have you seen what the rogue's done now?' He screwed the paper up and hurled it in the general direction of the bin.

Mrs Curtis picked the pages up calmly and smoothed them out. She hadn't read her horoscope on page 19 yet. The clergy were so selfish.

'He's only opened his own TV channel.'

'Oh dear.'

The good Father's reply was not suitable for gentle eyes to read. Suffice it to say the housekeeper blushed.

On RC101, the 'Save 'Em All' station, 'Pastor' John Mulvaney, ex-drunk, ex-gambler, ex-womaniser—officially anyway—called to the masses.

'If you think you're worth savin', if you think I'm worth savin', if you want people like us in heav'n, send your money now, folks. Your pledges will keep heav'n pure, and y'all know what I mean by that, doncha?'

He winked lasciviously at camera six. Behind him the bank of phones threatened to overheat with use. His fifth wife, Cherry-Marie smiled prettily at the camera, her perfect 19-year-old's face at odds with her less-than-perfect 38-year-old's body. Pastor John fingered the cleft in his chin and realised how sexy the intern college girl Leanne was. He'd have to do something there soon. Six was his lucky number.

Twin boys, each with a cleft, are hardly likely to go the same way. Forget horoscopes. It's all in the etymology.

Untouchable?—Polly Caley

'I prefer cold hands and a warm heart.' He laughed nervously, adding soundlessly, 'Seriously fellas, I'll wager there's a deal to be done here.'

But he couldn't stop a legion of smouldering palms from clawing and tugging, intent on dragging his soul into their molten pit.

In life, he was ruthless—powerfully grabbing whatever and whoever he chose. Yet here he lay, fiery fingers mauling him relentlessly.

And he had no dirt on these faceless fiends to bargain with. If he could've moved, he'd have gnashed his teeth, thrown punches their way and spat orders to the bulk of highly trained security flanking his bedside. Those boys sure as hell could unleash a fatal pounding on these sulphurous skulls.

But he was motionless, voiceless and these blazing bastards were all over him.

The finest cotton of Egypt lay cool and crisp beneath him and the temperature of this whole private wing was set for his comfort; yet he was conscious of a searing, burning ripping through the morphine fog, right through his chest.

Surely this torso attack would register on the cutting-edge technology he was hooked up to. And surely this roomful of the highest paid, Harvard professionals would be alerted to take immediate action.

Heads would roll if somebody didn't act NOW!

But the room remained largely silent. Monitors hummed and beeped. The white coats murmured occasionally as they quietly moved about their business, updating charts, unhurried.

Seeing his own ample, unmoving mass on the bed, for the first time he wondered if he felt sorry. It was a new state. He wanted to weep into his mother's lap. What if this godawful heat was finally the tug of guilt? Maybe if he was sorry enough—and truly sorry about all of it—he'd have a chance.

Vampire Wedding in North Cornwall—Mark Kilburn

The rock face had a sheen to it, filtering the moon so the rough sea sparkled.

High in the hills we left our otherworld for the wedding of an actor long-since dead.

Miss Carstairs arrived in her horse-drawn carriage and mingled uncertainly, an ivory crucifix secreted between her breasts.

The groom introduced his bride to Mr Crowley of Tregerthen—snarled when he tried to seduce her with a love-apple.

I was nervous and you soothed my fevered brow, whispered: 'It's an unforgiving situation.'

Reverend Ghost, sucking a cantaloupe, said: 'The bride, you know—I had her once. She's to die for.'

The wedding cake was a monster—a marzipan castle set in a Transylvanian forest, a sugary quatrain written in the frozen water of the moat.

After the ceremony we made our way to the Red Corpuscle Bar where Igor fixed us gangrene on the rocks. The ocean raged and we raised a toast of vodka and quince—danced through the night to the Bongo Pass Trio.

I flirted with an acolyte of the Dark Count, asked you to forgive me this temporary sin.

I could feel the tension as the not-so-happy couple cut the cake. The bride licked her buttery fangs and smeared fresh ruby lipstick along the folds of her black dress.

At twilight a horse drawn hearse clattered the newly-weds along winding dusky roads to Madam Trevelyan's honeymoon crypt.

The fields were frosted and we covered our eyes; splinters of morningtide encroached like a fateful deceit.

Miss Carstairs emerged from the shadows, surrounded by her baying hunters. Father Tremayne led the procession of light, singing 'Onward Christian Soldiers'. They pointed their hawthorn stakes at us with contempt, held their crucifixes high, emptied chamber after chamber of silver bullets—their wedding gift at dawn.

Where are you Going? Can I Come?—Claire Llewellyn

You rescued me eight months ago from a miserable room. It was small, cold; I was lonely but not alone in my plight. I was so happy you chose me, I heard you say that I rescued you too from a similar fate. We were made for each other, inseparable. My love was unconditional, and when you told me that I was such a good girl, gave me treats and rubbed my belly, I thought your love would always be…

One day you put on your coat, walked to the door, I followed—where was my lead? I sat, barking to remind you. You looked down at me, patted my head: 'Sorry, girl, gotta go back to the office.' I ran to the window and watched as you drove away. The vehicle that had once brought us together was now tearing us apart! I cried, I howled, I was so distraught I peed myself. We did not take our usual morning walk. I was alone again, abandoned!

I ran upstairs to your room and removed your bed covers, seeking out your scent. I rolled around, but was not soothed. I dived into a hamper of clothes to absorb your essence, yet no solace I found. Maybe food would calm me, but my bowl was empty! I jumped up at the counter, reaching for whatever was there. I chewed a bit of this and that, nothing that tasted good. Then you returned; joy of joys…

'What the ****! BAD girl!' Harsh words replaced the comfort I had known as you toured the house. 'This isn't going to work!' You were at the door again, this time with my lead. Reunited in that vehicle, until we stopped and you left me!

Writing in the Wendy House—
Martin Driscoll

So I finally got the kid s to play a boardgame having peeled them away from the Disney+ channel and got my husband to finish off the fiendish bits of blue sky, or water, (who can tell?) on the thousand piece puzzle that has dominated the dining table for a bleedin' fortnight—I expect we shall find the remnants of those peas every time it comes back out of the box…

So, kids sorted, check.

Hubby engaged, check.

Dog gone for long walk with mum, check.

At last, I can open the large envelope that contains:

MY FINISHED FIRST NOVEL!

I had worked like a demon in the only place of refuge I could find where I might stay undisturbed for a while, Lisa's Wendy House, grandly titled in my head as my 'A room of one's own' in homage to the divine Virginia, half hour's here and there until the household tracked me down.

I tore at the flap, shook the crisp virgin book out into my shaking hands and admired the fine tooling of the embossed cover lettering, the super graphic designer's jacket art, the cool, the elegant Garamond font and open-spaced justified lines; I thought of the time and money poured into it by the editors, and publishers, truly it looked a thing of beauty.

Sadly, I am a very bad writer and the book is rubbish.

Authors' Biographies

Claire Fluff Llewellyn (professional name) Born in Worcester, England, Claire Llewellyn, (affectionately known as 'Fluff'), is a writer/poet/actress/film maker. She is poetically inspired by the works of Edgar Allan Poe and Roald Dahl. She moved to the States to pursue a musical career, but became a horror film maker instead.
Contact email: flufflewellyn@gmail.com

Fritz Cavelle After a successful career on the building-sites of Birmingham Fritz travelled the world as an IT consultant before spending a decade as a trainee hermit in a deconsecrated church in Worcester. He is now employed as an apprentice sod-buster in North-West France, under the benevolent gaze of an organic French Hippy and the malevolent glare of a deranged feral cat.

Hedy Lewis hails from Shipley Gate, Nottinghamshire, roughly as far away from the sea as you can get. Her rural existence is marred by the lack of decent broadband, which is the only reason she writes. She keeps two small humans and a small army of goats alive, come the zombie apocalypse she's not sure which will be more useful.

Helen Beckett lives in Cardiff. She has tried to use her 'lockdown' time productively, learning to speak Welsh, finishing her supernatural novel and writing flash fictions. Her next goal is to put to paper the romantic suspense story which is currently whirring around in her head.

Jacqui Gillespie lives in North Gloucestershire. Her first published non-fiction book was in collaboration with two other authors, *Aspects of Community Life in the Great War*. She has now branched out into fiction, which she says is great fun and brings out her imaginative side.

James Mason has been, in very small and superficial ways, a poet, comedian, editor and copywriter. He lives in Worcester but is a born and bred Cornishman, a fact he will shoehorn into any conversation, at any opportunity. He has small amounts of published work dotted around the place.

Jamie D Stacey is a part-time writer and full-time father. An avid writer of flash fiction and aspiring novelist (finalising that debut), he is drawn to stories that empathise, encourage, and empower.
Find him on Twitter @JamieDStacey1 and Medium @staceyjamied

Jan Baynham, from Cardiff, had two novels published by Ruby Fiction in 2020; her third will be out in September 2021. Her first collection of short stories was published in 2019. Follow her on her Jan Baynham Writer Facebook page and on Twitter @JanBaynham where she runs a fortnightly writing blog, https://janbaynham.blogspot.com.

Johnny 'Mogs' Morris mainly writes poetry, but does dabble in prose and even play writing. He regularly performs his poetry at open mic events and is a member of two writing groups based in Stourbridge in the West Midlands. In 2017 Black Pear Press published his first book of poetry called *Poems Your Parents Won't Like.* His children's novel, *Griff*, was published in 2018.
For more info check out his website:
http://johnnymogs.co.uk/

Joy Ryland has taken early retirement after spending her working life in finance. She has a passion for writing and is trying desperately to finish her first novel. Her other interests are walking her dog and wild swimming when the water warms up.

Kate Jones is a retired teacher and has lived in Worcester for approximately 30 years. She has always written stuff since a child and particularly enjoys flash fiction and poetry, the sillier the better. She has decided it's about time she did something with it.

Kevin Brooke writes mainly for young people and is the Young Writer Ambassador at Worcestershire Litfest. He has two books published by Black Pear Press, namely, *Jimmy Cricket* and *Max & Luchia: The Game Makers*. A third book, *The Objectors,* is due to be published in 2021. He is also known to dress up as a Knight and tell stories as a 'Story Knight'.

Leena Batchelor is a Worcester-based poet and spoken word artist, finding inspiration in travels around the UK and watching life whilst sipping over the rim of a teacup. Leena's writings provide tools for everyday life and an antidote to the vitriolic rhetoric pervading society.

Lisa Johnston is a poet and creative community project co-ordinator with Red Bucket Projects. She has work published in many anthologies and has just released her first collection of poetry with photography, *Heart Lines and Life Lines*, through Dream Well Publishing. For more information about Red Bucket Projects please go to www.redbucketprojects.com or email Lisa at redbucketprojects@gmail.com

Mark Kilburn was born in Birmingham. Literary prizes include: a Canongate award for new fiction (2001); winner, AbcTales poetry competition (2012); and first place in the Cerasus Poetry Olympics competition (2020). His novel, *Hawk Island*, is available from electronpress.com and his poetry collection, *Beautiful Fish*, is available from Amazon.

Martin Driscoll Still writing, still amazed when anything gets published, still hoping the bar gets lowered further each year; if you are reading this in 2021 then it just happened again! As a purely visual and graphics based man, to be recognised for his wordsmith's skills simply beggars belief, one day he might actually make some money out of it—dream on!

Paul Johnson Aged 60 and with his wealth and health receding faster than his hairline Paul realised his only option was to become a legend, so, and in the absence of any obvious writing skills he swore to 'poke and provoke' whilst at all times chasing that elusive beast, the sublime.

Polly Caley This may not be 29 Acacia Road, but this is Polly—the schoolchildren's mum who leads an exciting double life. For when Polly picks up a pen, an amazing transformation occurs. Polly is not Bananaman, but is ever alert for the call to fiction. Please do look out for her.

Polly Stretton is a writer and poet. Her work has been widely published in anthologies and collections of her poetry are published by Black Pear Press. Polly's first collection *Girl's Got Rhythm* was followed by a series of poems about the tragic young poet *Chatterton*, and *The Alchemy of 42*.

Roz Levens Fresh from the success of her accomplished one-woman Zoom show 'why not take advantage of lockdown and teach yourself the bagpipes—and other courtroom dramas', Roz Levens lives in Devon and is attempting to write the ultimate novel. For a few weeks more, she is still Worcestershire Literary Festival's Flash Fiction Slam champion (for the 3rd time)…

Safia Sawal lives with her partner, dog and cat in North Worcestershire. She has been attending a writing class and workshops for a number of years, she finds the supportive network encouraging, inspiring and challenging. When she is not working, writing or drinking tea she is walking her dog in the woods.

Seraphim Bryant is a graduate of the University of Worcester. Part of the 'Story Knights'; a collaboration delivering workshops to encourage independent writing and creativity in young people. Seraphim is a freelance illustrator and writes young adult novels and short stories. She is also a regular at 42 Worcester spoken-word club.

Sue St. John lives in Herefordshire enjoying a spot of country living after life in the big smoke. A career in marketing, copy checking for others, followed by a chance win in a fun fiction competition, Sue's writing debut comes at a later age and digs deep into past experiences as the basis for her fiction. Once a runner now a confirmed walker—dogs, golf, Nordic walking and plenty of walking to and from the allotment.

Susan Howe's short stories and flash fictions have been published and placed in competitions many times. A proud but displaced Yorkshirewoman, brevity is in her DNA.